Baby Baby

by

Viv French

First published in 2002 in Great Britain by
Barrington Stoke Ltd, Sandeman House, Trunk's Close,
55 High Street, Edinburgh EH1 1SR
www.barringtonstoke.co.uk

Reprinted 2005

ISBN 1-84299-061-6

Printed in Great Britain by Bell & Bain Ltd

A Note from the Author

It's very hard coping with a new baby at any age – I know, I've had four – but it's particularly difficult when you're very young and on your own. It doesn't make it any easier when society judges you without knowing all the facts. As April says in the book, "Put your hand up if you never made a mistake." How many of us could truthfully do that? Not me, I know.

I've worked in two units for schoolgirl mothers, and both times I learnt far more than the girls did. There are some fantastic teenage mums out there in the world. This book is in celebration of their bravery, their love for their babies, and their determination to do the very best for them. It comes with my love and thanks.

For Nancy

Contents

Chapter 1

The Beginning:
Pinkie and April

My heart is pounding and thundering and battering the walls of my chest. It's going to burst through my ribs any second. I'm going to explode. There'll be me, Pinkie, splattered all over the walls. Little sparkles and flashes burst inside my eyes, but there's blackness swirling round the outside of me. It's a huge blackness waiting to gulp me up ...

And the sea of faces in front of me is growing and growing. Thousands and thousands of faces with gaping mouths and huge eyes – and the eyes are staring at me – and I'm frozen. I can't move. I can't speak and the eyes are swaying ... to and fro ... to and ...

What?

Something's happening.

April's there beside me. She's pushed me onto a chair at the edge of the stage, and dumped Lee in my arms. I nearly drop him – it's my arms that clutch his little, warm, wriggly body, not me.

But it jolts me. I snatch a gasping breath. Lee wriggles again, and I hold him tightly. It's for my sake, not his.

Then I hear her. April. She's talking – and her voice isn't the way I've ever heard April sound. She sounds angry. And the dizziness clears away from my head and my eyes and I see her, and I see what she's doing.

She's standing in the middle of the platform and she's talking to those eyes. All those blank faces. She looks so skinny and pathetic in her sparkly little top and her bare stomach showing like chicken flesh and her spotless jeans and her snow-white trainers and – yes, I knew it. She's shaking back her hair. But she's talking. And I begin to hear what she's saying.

****

"Look at us," April says. "Me and Pinkie. Look at Pinkie. She's the one on the chair, the one with the baby. It's not her baby, it's mine. Pinkie's baby's in hospital. He's really, really ill, and Pinkie's been slogging to and fro to see him, and he's not getting any better.

"She's worn out. That's why she's not talking to you. It's not because she's scared of you. Pinkie's the bravest person I've ever met, and she's not scared of anything.

"It's me who's the scared one. I was so scared of having a baby I didn't sleep for weeks and weeks. It was only when I found out Pinkie was having a baby too that I began to sleep again.

"Why? Because Pinkie wasn't scared. She stuck out her stomach like she was proud, and that made me feel different. She was like a queen who's got all her money and her jewels and the very best kingdom in all the world stuffed inside her, and she wanted us all to know just how good she felt. I never got to be proud, but I stopped being so scared."

April stops for a minute, and I can see her biting her lip. Then the hair goes *flip* and she's talking again.

"I'm doing this all wrong," she says. "Pinkie wouldn't do it like this. But you're going to have to put up with me."

April stops again, and takes a breath. Her fists are clenched behind her back. The knuckles are white.

"I know exactly why we've been asked here," April says. "We're meant to be telling you how awful it is that we've had babies when we're only fifteen, and THEY," April looks across at the teachers lining the edges of the hall, "want us to tell you that it's all dreadful and you shouldn't have sex ever, ever until you're ancient just in case you end up like us. Why? Because we're dirt. That's what they think.

"We're the girls people look at and suck in their lips and shake their heads at. Or they say things like, 'taking your little brother for a walk?' when they just KNOW that those babies belong to us. They just want to hear us say it so they can feel good inside that they're not like we are. BAD girls."

There's a pause for a second.

"Do you know something? Something terrible?" April's voice is wobbling. "They think that Pinkie deserved what she got. A little, ill baby with tubes stuck down his throat and a plastic fish tank all round him. Well, I think people who think like that are *evil*. *They're* much, MUCH worse than we are. We made a mistake, and everybody does that sometimes."

April takes a step towards the edge of the platform. "That's true, isn't it? *Isn't it?* Put your hand up if you've never made a mistake. Go on! Show me!"

6

No-one moves.

"And nobody EVER deserves to have an ill baby. ESPECIALLY not someone like Pinkie."

****

April stamps her foot and wipes her eyes with the back of her hand and I know that she's crying. But it doesn't stop her. She digs deep into her jeans pocket, and because she's April she pulls out this little, neatly folded, clean white tissue. She blows her nose. And then she goes on talking.

And I think, who is this girl? Who's this April standing up in front of a hall full of kids and teachers and firing words at them as if she wanted to kill them?

It's not the April I see every day at the Centre. That April never speaks unless she's spoken to. April the goody-goody who always does her homework, who always keeps Lee spit clean and tidy, who helps clear up at the end of every school day.

And it's not the April I knew before that, the stuck-up townie girl who hung about in Park Street with all her naff friends. April, who was always flipping her hair, and showing off. April who thought she was SO much better than me, and couldn't stop letting me know it.

Well, until I told her.

But this April? I don't know her.

And I think all the way back to the beginning. To the first time I saw April.

8

Chapter 2
College Green

It was Phil who pointed April out.

We were sitting on College Green, Phil and me, at the time. We used to hang out there a lot, and all our friends did too. It was like being part of a big family – or better than a family. We all liked each other.

The Green is a big square of grass in the centre of town, and kids like us go there when they've got time off school, or college, or work, or it's the weekend – or if they haven't got anything else to do. We chat, and smoke, and every now and then someone has something a bit more interesting to pass round – you know what I mean? And if we've got any cash, we'll drink.

Anyway, it was a Saturday, and Phil and I were sitting on the Green and chatting to my mate, Rosie. She'd just had another piercing done, in her lip this time, and she was squinting at it in my little mirror. Phil was clicking his tongue stud against his teeth and telling her she ought to have her eyebrow done as well, when all these townie kids went strolling past.

"Look!" Phil said, and he laughed. "Why don't you ask them what they think, Rosie? Ask that little skinny one at the end – Little Miss Perfect!"

And we looked, and he was right. That girl was so squeaky clean she looked as if she'd just stepped out of a Barbie box.

Her hair was long and straight and shiny blonde, and she kept flipping it away from her face with a little pink hand with perfect nail-varnished nails. Her skin was a perfect plastic pink and didn't have a zit or a mark on it. Her clothes were so new-looking I expected to see price tags hanging off her bum.

"Mummy's little pet," I said. "Oooh! I bet Mummy wouldn't want to see her down here with us!"

Phil laughed again. "You're just jealous, Pinkie."

I snorted, and Rosie cackled.

Normally the townies didn't bother with the Green. They didn't want to mix with people like us – they called us goths, or punks, or talked loudly about grunge whenever they saw us.

They'd never ever EVER have dyed their hair jet black like Rosie, or bright pink like me, and they'd have died before they wore anything other than sparkly, little tops and fresh, clean jeans and snow-white trainers.

Well, the girls wore things like that – the boys wore what they thought were trendy sweatshirts or T-shirts with naff logos on them. And they all hung out in the coffee bars up Park Street, drinking non-stop coffee and laughing Aren't-We-Clever laughs.

They were SO not cool.

Little Miss Perfect and her group strolled on past us. All us lot went very quiet, and stared at them, and you could see them beginning to twitch a bit. They couldn't give in, though. They had to face us out and pretend they didn't notice we were watching.

They did it to show off – you could tell. They thought they were SO brave – I mean, they probably thought we were all off our heads with vodka and drugs, and likely to bite them or spit on them or infect them with some deadly disease just by looking at them.

The girls were doing a lot of giggling. One of them looked at my biker boots and said something to the girl next to her, and they both sniggered.

Little Miss Perfect gave me a sort of pitying smile. She was holding hands with an oily-looking geek with a smarmy sneer, and he didn't look at me at all.

"Come on, April dahling," he said. "Let's go grab a cawfee."

And then they were gone. But it was odd. That was the first time I'd ever seen April, but after that I kept noticing her – she seemed to pop up wherever I went. I'd be walking down the hill to the Green, and she'd be walking up. I'd be coming out of the chip shop with my cheesy chips, and she'd be going in. When I went to the job centre she was outside looking at the board.

I even saw her once in the London Road, and believe you me that is NOT a place where I'd expect to see someone like her. It hasn't got any shiny-pink-fluffy-bunny silver ribbon shops anywhere – it's mostly charity shops or empty windows full of old letters and dead flies. And people sleeping under old blankets in shop doorways.

Mum says it's disgusting, but I go for the charity shops. You can get good stuff there if you hunt about a bit. And there's a shop called Silver Tiger where I buy my hair dye. And I look at the clothes and wish I had more money so as I could buy the long, black, velvet skirt at the end of the rail – it's been there for ages and I keep hoping they'll reduce it but they don't.

Anyway – I was coming out of Silver Tiger and there she was – looking in the window! And she gave me that pathetic, little, pitying smile again, and flipped her hair back so as I could see how clean and perfect she was.

I just walked straight past her. I heard her make some kind of little puffing noise – I expect she was trying not to breathe the same air as me. I didn't look back. I walked on down the road to where I was meeting Phil in the Chinese chippy.

It began to get to me.

After that time I saw her in the London Road, she was around even more. Everywhere I went, there she'd be. Sometimes she was on her own, and sometimes she was with the geek. He looked right through me, and that was easy to deal with. That happens to me all the time. It happens to me at home. It comes with the image – people either look through you, or raise their eyebrows and stare – and make some stupid comment.

But April? There was something weird about her, something that made me notice when she turned up.

OK.

Sometimes after she'd gone twinkling past me, I'd find myself looking at my hands.

Why?

I don't know. But I'd suddenly see that my black nail varnish was chipped and my nails were dirty. I'd see that my silver stud wristbands were dull and grubby. I'd see that my jacket cuffs were fraying, and there were stains on the sleeves. And although I knew that was the way I was, and I'd chosen to be that way, and I *liked* being that way, it was different. It was like looking into a twisted glass. Like looking into those dead, fly-filled windows in the empty shops in the London Road. I felt sleazy. Like Mum was always saying. Dirty. Grubby.

It made me do odd things – things I wouldn't normally have done. I still wasn't quite certain if I thought Phil was God Almighty or a minging git, but when April was around, I'd really come on to him. Just to show her. I'd grab his bum, and wriggle up right against him, and force my tongue down his throat.

Why?

I don't know. You tell me.

It ended up with me having full-on sex with Phil. And it was April's fault.

Does that sound mad?

Probably.

But it was after I'd had a go at her. Sworn at her.

I told her just what I thought about her following me, sneering at me, thinking she was better than me.

She didn't answer back. She just stared at me, and twisted her hands round and round.

And she was so pathetic that her eyes filled up with tears. Crybaby. Mummy's girl.

I don't often do stuff like that – swearing at people. But April was getting on my nerves so much I had to.

But do you know what?

It didn't make me feel any better.

Afterwards I felt so chewed up inside that when Phil said, "My mum's away for the night," I didn't even think twice. I never cry, but I had to do something to get away from that feeling. To cover it up. To make it go away.

We went back to Phil's place, and all the time I was thinking, I bet that little stuck-up bitch doesn't do THIS, so I let Phil do stuff I've always said Piss-Off-You-Must-Be-Joking to before.

OK – we'd had sex before. Made love. Whatever you want to call it. And I'd had a good time …

But this was different.

Fast. Angry. Rough stuff.

I never even got round to making sure Phil used a condom. So he didn't.

Chapter 3
Park Street

Do you want to know about the very first time Pinkie actually spoke to me?

It was awful.

We were outside the chippy – not the Chinese chippy in the London Road, but the one at the bottom of Park Street. I'd seen Pinkie go in, and I stood outside and told myself that if I counted to 50 and she still hadn't come out then I'd go away. But she came out just as I got to 44, so I did it.

I took a deep breath and I smiled at her and I said, "Hi!" And I was SO pleased with myself because I'd finally made myself say something.

Me, April.

I'd said HI! to Pinkie ...

And she swore at me.

She asked me why I'd been following her. She said I'd been sneering at her and showing off for weeks, and she wasn't going to take any more of it. She said I was a stuck-up little bitch and why didn't I go and **** my oily geek of a boyfriend. (I still can't use that word, even though I've been trying and trying. It still sounds wrong when I say it.)

22

She said she knew I thought she was dirt but she had every right to be the way she was, and she wasn't going to change for anyone, and I could go to hell and rot there as far as she cared. And then she sort of flung herself at her boyfriend and they went off down the road all over each other.

Why?

Why did she think all those things?

Didn't she know that I thought she was amazing?

Yes, I had been following her. Just a bit. And only because she was so – I don't know how to put it. So different. So much herself. I wanted to see what someone like her did. It was like seeing into a different world, a world where people do what THEY want, and not what everyone else wants them to do.

Look at Pinkie's clothes. Right from the first moment I saw her I thought they were beautiful. All those different swirly skirts, and velvets, and that silver studdy thing she wears round her wrist.

And her hair. I'd never seen hair like that. It was pink – BRIGHT pink – like some lovely flower from a place I'd never ever been. It stood up in little spikes on her head, and then there were long bits trailing down her back.

It was Pinkie's own way of being and no-one, NO-ONE in the whole wide world was like her. She had this stud in her nose, and another on her lip, and they glittered in the sunshine, and it was as if all of her was saying I don't care what you think. I'm ME, and you can like it or lump it. And it made me feel like one of those throwaway silver paper fairies you put on the top of the Christmas tree, and I could see that all the people I hung about with were the same.

And then I thought, that's right. We WERE all the same. And I began to feel weird inside. It was like I didn't really exist, like I wasn't anything more than that paper fairy. If someone looked at me from the side I wouldn't be there.

But Pinkie – she was REAL. And I began to try to be where I knew she'd be, so I could stare at her and see what realness was like.

And then I had this idea that I wanted to be her friend.

That sounds so silly. It's like when I was at nursery, when we all had bestest friends.

But it wasn't silly to me. I just wanted to know what it was like to be her – to be able to laugh with a whole lot of friends while you sat on the grass and smoked and drank. Not to be always afraid of saying the wrong thing, or liking the wrong band, or not wearing the right clothes, or asking for milky coffee when everyone knows it's called *café latte*.

When I was with Marco and the others, I was always sitting on the edge of my seat and watching to see that I got things right. I watched so hard it hurt. I kind of listened with every little bit of me to see what was the right thing to say, what wouldn't make them stare at me.

Sometimes when I said something they'd look at Marco for a second, and I could see this tiny, secret message flashing from one to the other, but it wasn't my message. Not a message to me.

No.

It was a message about me.

It was a doesn't-she-KNOW-she's-a-total-and-utter-wannabe-and-will-never-NEVER-make-it kind of message.

I wondered what Pinkie would do if she'd been me, but I knew that someone like her just wouldn't care what other people thought.

And she was – I couldn't think how to put it – she was too BIG to bother about putting someone down. She wouldn't mind if someone had different ideas. She'd LIKE it. I'd heard her arguing on College Green, arguing and shouting and then falling about laughing because her friend Rosie liked Robbie Williams and she thought that was SO sad – but it didn't make her not like her friend any more.

So I thought, I'd like a friend like that.

I tried smiling at her, but she didn't seem to see me. Not really. And I wasn't surprised.

Once I even went to the London Road because that's where all the punk shops are, and I was even thinking that maybe – just maybe – I might have a look at the clothes in Silver Tiger. And then I saw Pinkie inside, and I thought NOW!!! NOW I can say hello because Marco isn't here, and SHE'S on her own and maybe we could talk and then go and have a coffee or something.

But I couldn't do it.

I just made a sort of puffing noise and she rushed past me as if she was in a hurry and I was left standing there. And I had this wild, mad idea that maybe I'd go and buy clothes like Pinkie and dye my hair and then I could join the College Green kids.

But I couldn't.

I couldn't even go into the shop. It was too dark. And it smelt ... weird. And I was scared.

So I went back to Park Street, back to Marco and the crowd. They didn't look up when I walked in. They hadn't really noticed I'd gone.

But I didn't stop thinking about Pinkie ... and the way she was.

Chapter 4
Underground Car Park

Round about that time something strange began to happen.

Marco saw I wasn't thinking about him as much as he wanted, and he began to be quite nice to me.

That was odd.

Usually I was careful to listen to everything he said and smiled and laughed a lot at his jokes even if I didn't think they were funny. I did that because he said I was lucky to have him and he could easily find someone else. I didn't know what I would do if that happened – I suppose I was scared of being on my own. Everyone in our crowd was a two. They laughed at people on their own. Especially the girls.

But now I was thinking about Pinkie, Marco began to pay me more attention. He held my hand more, and that was OK – but he tried touching me up more as well.

I didn't like it that much, I never have. Usually when he did things like that I'd wriggle away and talk about something at school or say I wasn't feeling well, and he'd get cross and say there was something wrong with me. And he wouldn't talk to me for a bit.

But now something changed, and he stopped being angry when I pushed him off. He went on trying, though. More and more.

And I went on thinking about being like Pinkie.

I got it into my head that if I was more like Pinkie, if Pinkie was my friend, then maybe I could tell Marco I didn't really like him that much. And maybe I could stop going round with all the same people. Maybe – and my insides did strange little hops when I even thought of it – I could be one of Pinkie's friends and just be me. *If* there was a me, that is. I wasn't sure that there was.

And one night it happened.

I was with Marco and the others and they began talking about Pinkie's friends on College Green. They called them crusty goths, and dirty punks, and they were saying they were sure all the girls were slags and were talking about what would it be like to sleep with them. And Marco said he thought they'd catch some horrible disease if they did.

Something went TWANG! inside me, and I said, "I'm going to get some chips", and I got up and walked out of the coffee bar and went down the road to the chip shop.

I heard Marco calling, "Get me some too, baby!" but I didn't turn round. As I went I was muttering to myself, "I'm going to say hello. I really, really am. I am." And at that moment I really thought I could.

And when I got to the chippy I saw Pinkie inside, and it was as if this was all meant to happen. There was a picture inside my head, and it was SO clear it was more real than the steamy window and the smell of oily fat and the feel of the pavement under my feet.

It was a picture of Pinkie coming out, and me saying, HI! and Pinkie smiling and saying HI! back. And then the picture was of us sharing chips together on the bench by the Green and Pinkie saying to all the others, Hey! This is April! She's come to be one of us now!

It was so real I began to smile.

But then I saw Pinkie reach out to pay for her chips, and my stomach flipped over. I decided to count to 50, and if she didn't come out by the end of 50, I'd go away.

But I got to 44 and she did.

So I said, "Hi!"

And she swore at me.

I just stood there. My throat had such a huge lump in it I couldn't swallow. I felt sick and my stomach was whirling and flapping and my legs were so wobbly I had to hang onto the chip shop doorway.

When Marco arrived a bit later I cried all over him. I didn't mean to but I couldn't stop. He couldn't understand why I was crying and he took me back to his car and drove down the road and into the underground car park. He turned off the engine and kept trying to kiss me and stroke me and pat me. And I still couldn't stop crying.

And do you know what?

He didn't ask me what it was that was making me cry. That made me cry even more. I'd had this nasty little feeling deep down inside me for ages – a feeling that he didn't really care about me as *me* at all – and now I knew it was true. I was just – what do you call it? Arm candy. A trophy. He didn't

give a toss about what was making me cry.
He just wanted to slide his slimy, hot hands
under my top and down inside my knickers
like he always tried to, and he thought
because I was crying over him it meant he
could go as far as he wanted and I wouldn't
mind.

No.

He didn't care if I minded or not. He just
didn't want me to make a fuss. If I wasn't
saying NO then it meant I was saying YES ...
so he went on and on.

I went on crying. And all the time he was
undoing my jeans and pulling at my bra and
pushing me down on the seat, I was crying,
and inside my head all these pictures were
clicking up like a weird sort of film. It was as
if what was happening to the outside of me,
the pushing and the grunting and the heavy,

sweaty breathing – well, that wasn't really happening at all.

What was real were those pictures in my head.

Picture 1: Pinkie swearing at me.

Picture 2: A little glob of spit on her chin.

Picture 3: Her eyes cold and glassy staring right into me.

Picture 4: Me standing with my mouth half open and my hands clutching each other.

The last picture was the worst of all. It was the inside picture, the picture inside my head. The picture of sitting around and laughing with Pinkie and being a real person. I saw how stupid it was. I saw my stupid ideas fade and die. And I could see myself the way Pinkie saw me. I was nothing.

I don't know how long it was before Marco rolled off me. At the time it didn't seem to matter — nothing mattered just then.

He drove me home without saying anything at all, and didn't get out of the car when we got to my front door. I didn't say anything either. I got my key out of my bag and let myself in, and I heard the car roaring away down the road.

Mum was sitting watching telly with Mrs Barton from the top floor flat.

Mrs Barton turned round and smiled at me and said, "Hello, April dear," but Mum went on watching someone putting a plant in a hole in the ground.

Then Mum said, "I can't think why people make such a fuss about gardening." She smoothed her hair back. "All that nasty mud and mess."

"But it's lovely when you see the flowers growing," Mrs Barton told her. "I couldn't do without my window boxes."

Mum didn't answer. She does that when she doesn't agree with someone else's point of view. She thinks arguments are like gardening. Messy.

She and Mrs Barton sat in silence for a moment while some big girl in welly boots stamped the earth down around the plant, and then Mum said, "Could you put the kettle on, please, April? Unless you're too tired after having fun all day."

So I put on the kettle and made them tea – ordinary for Mrs Barton, and pale, golden Earl Grey for Mum with a thin slice of lemon – and then I went to bed.

At about three in the morning it suddenly hit me. I'd had sex. I could be pregnant. And I was so scared I could hardly breathe.

Chapter 5
Tinley Road

It was Miss Hathaway who told me.
She didn't know she was telling me, of course.
Silly cow.

We were supposed to be changing for PE,
and as always I hadn't got my kit. I used the
usual old excuse about it being a bad time of
the month.

Miss Hathaway said, "Pinkie – you of all
people need to take some exercise. You've
really put on weight. You'll have people thinking

you're pregnant!" And then she laughed, and the nerds who think Miss Hathaway is the best all sniggered, and went charging off to swing on ropes and stuff.

I didn't think much about it to begin with. I sat down on the bench with the others – there were always at least six or seven of us who couldn't be bothered with climbing up wall bars and beefing about.

Carla started some long and boring story about what she'd been up to the night before, and I began to loosen the buttons on my skirt because it felt tight … and then I stopped.

What had Miss Hathaway said?

Pregnant?

Stuff that.

But then again …

I began to add things up.

My clothes. I didn't want to think they were tight – but it was true. My jeans wouldn't do up at all.

There was the sick bug that had gone on for nearly a month. But I'd only felt sick in the evenings, I told myself. It was morning sickness you got if you were pregnant, wasn't it?

And then there was the long gap since my last period. That often happened with me. But how long had it really been? I counted backwards.

I could remember pinching Mum's tampons, and her shouting at me for it. As usual. As always. But when was that? One month ago? Two months? No – it was before that ...

And one last thing. That time I did it with Phil at his house. When his mum was away. When ...

I swallowed hard, and leant back on the wall behind the bench. It was very odd. I was having this weird WEIRD feeling. A bit of it was panic, and cold, clammy fear – but mostly it was a sort of – pride. That's the only word I can think of to describe it.

I was having a baby.

It was there, somewhere inside me.

A tiny person, and it was mine. And I put both my hands over my stomach as if I was protecting it, loving it already. My baby. MINE.

By the time I'd scraped up enough money to buy the pregnancy test I knew I didn't need it. It wasn't going to tell me anything I didn't

already know. I'd worked it all out for myself.
I was having a baby, and it would arrive in
May. I'd made something totally and completely
amazing – a whole new person. And wild
horses weren't going to stop me keeping it.

Mum made me take another test. She didn't
want to believe it was true, although she said
it was no more than she'd expected of me.
Then she tried really hard to make me have
an abortion, but I wouldn't listen. I was
already madly in love with this strange little
thing growing and growing inside me.

Mum shouted and yelled, and my step-dad
Nick sighed and went to the pub even more
than usual. My three little step-sisters
stared at me as if I was a freak. Mum said I'd
ruined her life once before, and now I was
doing it again, and I said I didn't care.

I said I'd move out as soon as I could.
I went out and got an evening job washing up
in a café. I did it so I could save some money
to buy things for Zak.

That was what I was going to call him.

Zak.

I knew he was going to be a boy.

He and I were going to do things, go
places. He'd look at me and listen to me and
I'd tell him everything he wanted to know.
He'd love me more than anyone else in the
whole wide world, and I'd love him the same
way back.

I thought I'd be able to leave school and
get a full-time job until Zak was born, but I
wasn't allowed to. They said I had to go to
this centre. A sort of school, really –
The Tinley Road Centre for Schoolgirl Mothers.

I had to stay there until I was sixteen, and I had to do my exams, and that was the law. I was to start there as soon as a place became free, and I'd be allowed time off when I'd had the baby. There was a nursery there, and they'd look after Zak while I was in school.

I huffed and fussed about it, but I didn't really have any choice. In the end I said OK, I'd go, and the social worker fixed up the date I'd start.

And the day came when I was due to start at Tinley Road, and do you know what? I was actually excited. It meant that Zak was that bit nearer happening – although I knew he was well on his way already.

Quite a long time back I'd started getting these funny little flutters inside my belly. The hospital said he was moving – he was waving his little legs and arms about. I couldn't believe it when the nurse first told me. I'd been scared that he was dying or something.

By the time I went to Tinley Road, I was used to him bouncing about. I liked it. It was as if he was saying, Here I am! Don't forget I'm on the way!

I made a real effort that morning. You didn't have to wear uniform at the new place, so I reckoned I'd make a big entrance.

No.

WE'D make a big entrance – me and Zak. I twisted little pink feathers and sparkles into my hair, and I wore my best skirt and my black, sloppy sweater. It was lucky for me that I liked long skirts and loose tops. Although I couldn't do the skirt buttons up I could string elastic across my bulge, and cover it up with my sweater.

I looked just about the same as I always did. Then I pulled on my biker boots with the studs, and I felt great. Zak and me – we were on our way.

Mum sniffed as I walked past her to go out. "You won't have time for all those frilly skirts and huge boots when you've got a baby to look after," she said. "It's no fun being a teenage mother, you know."

I didn't answer, and she slammed the door behind me.

I didn't care. I strode down the road to the bus stop, and I found a seat right at the front on the top deck – my favourite place. I sang all the way to Tinley Road, and I rang the bell to stop the bus with a massive PING that made all the old biddies 'tut tut' to each other.

The Centre was two houses beyond the bus stop, and I shut the front gate behind me with a wonderful CLANG as I swung inside.

The teacher who met me at the door looked OK. She was dressed in jeans and a T-shirt, and she smiled at me as if she meant it. "You must be Pauline," she said.

I shook my head. "Everyone calls me Pinkie."

She looked at some papers that she had in her hand, and bit her lip as if she'd done something dreadful. "I'm so sorry," she said, "I should have noticed that. I'm called Liz, and I hate it when people call me Elizabeth. It sounds so ..." she stopped, and waved her arms in the air.

"Queen-like?" I suggested.

Liz laughed. "Maybe that's it. Anyway, you're Pinkie. I'll make sure it's changed on your notes. Come this way, and I'll introduce you to the others. There's thirteen of us at the moment, fourteen with you."

She showed me along a corridor and into a big room at the end where a load of girls were bent over tables piled high with books.

They looked up as I walked in.

And there she was.

April.

She had big, black shadows under her eyes, and her clothes weren't squeaky clean any more – but it was still the same April. Her trainers were still snow-white, and her nails were pink and shiny.

She was staring at me, and as she stared she flicked at her shiny, blonde hair with her hand.

And it brought it all back – how she used to follow me round, and how she'd made me feel somehow ashamed of myself. Uncomfortable. And how I'd take my feelings out on Phil ...

But then I thought of something else. If it hadn't been for April I wouldn't have done what I did that night in Phil's house ... and I wouldn't have Zak. So I thought, stuff her.

And then I thought, that's a joke! Someone already has!

Chapter 6
Hostel

I couldn't believe it when Pinkie walked into Tinley Road. They'd said someone new was coming, but they told us her name was Pauline. I was so surprised I couldn't say anything. I just stared.

She looked wonderful. Beautiful, really. Anyone could see she was pregnant – she was quite big – but she was glowing. Her hair was sparkly. There were little, pink feathers tucked into it. She looked as if she owned the world. She swirled into the room, and smiled at everyone.

Well, not everyone. Her eyes kind of whizzed past me as if I wasn't there.

Liz introduced us all. Cherry, Tanya, Hannah, Jem, Jackie – and the rest.

"This is Pinkie," Liz said. "Hope you'll make her feel welcome."

"Thought you said it was someone called Pauline," Jackie said.

Liz shook her head. "Mix-up in the office. Sorry."

Tanya was straight in. "How far gone are you?"

"Seven months," Pinkie said. "Almost."

That made me jump. I was almost seven months gone too. And it must have been about seven months since I last saw Pinkie –

at least, since I saw her face to face. Since she'd told me what she thought of me.

Pinkie was looking Tanya up and down. I held my breath. Tanya was tough, and she liked the rest of us to pay her what she called 'real respect'. She got SO angry if she thought anyone was taking the mick. I was dead scared of her – but then, I was scared of everything.

Pinkie was looking puzzled. "When's yours due?"

Tanya gave her a look, and the air went cold. "She's in the nursery."

"Whoops," Pinkie said, and she leant over and patted Tanya's arm. "Didn't mean you looked big or anything. I just thought we were all at the same stage."

I could see Tanya thinking, trying to decide if Pinkie was for real or not. And then she smiled, and slapped Pinkie's shoulder.

"Nah," Tanya said, "I'm out of here in two weeks' time. I'm sixteen on the 20th – and man! You won't see me and Jade for dust!"

Then Tanya pulled out the chair next to her, and Pinkie sat down, and before ten minutes was up you'd think they'd known each other for ever.

By breaktime Tanya had given Pinkie the low-down on everyone in the centre. Even me.

She jerked a thumb in my direction and told Pinkie, "That's April."

And I waited for Pinkie to say that she knew me, but she didn't. She just nodded as if she'd never set eyes on me before.

Tanya went on, "She's one of the hostel kids. They're the ones who've been chucked out of home. There's three of them at the moment. Her, Hannah and Jem."

Pinkie looked interested. She leant forward. "There's a hostel? Can anyone live there?"

Tanya shook her head. "Nah. Only if your mum or whoever signs something to say they don't want nothing to do with you ever again. The social go on trying, though – trying to get everyone back together." She giggled. "All happy families. Costs them less that way, don't it?"

Liz came in just then, and we had to get on with our maths. I could see Pinkie looking thoughtful, though, and once or twice she looked in my direction.

Later on, I heard her asking Liz about the hostel, but Liz told her the same as Tanya had.

Then Liz said, "It isn't all that nice, anyway. We do our best, but it really needs stripping down and repainting all through. Ask April about it. She's been living there for a couple of months now."

But Pinkie never asked me.

What would I have said if she had?

I suppose I'd have said that it was scary. It was cold at night, and it sounded as if the wind was banging against the building even if it wasn't. The rooms were painted a sicky sort of green, and the warden was a little old lady who spent most of her time knitting and chatting with the older women who lived there. I don't know why they were there. They didn't speak to me much.

Hannah and Jem had buddied up, and were in and out of each other's rooms all the time.

Hannah had had her baby, Dean, and he screamed all night long. She couldn't be bothered to get up and feed him more than once a night and Dean was always hungry, so he just went on crying.

Jem never woke up, but I couldn't sleep. I don't think I'd have slept much anyway. I was too scared. I felt as if a monster was growing inside me, as if I was being taken over.

I looked at Dean to see what a baby was like, and I hated him. Oh, I know all girls are supposed to love babies, but it's different when you've got one swelling you up and making you hideous. And Dean was always screaming. He never seemed to stop. It went on echoing in my ears even when Hannah was feeding him and he was slurping and squelching.

And I was terrified of what would happen when it was time for the thing inside me to come out. Would it hurt? What was it like?

I'd seen babies being born in films on the TV, and there was always so much shrieking and yelling, and often the mothers died. I didn't want to die. I don't know why I didn't, because everything was awful, but I didn't.

When I did sleep I had nightmares.

I was on this long, long road and I knew I wasn't ever going to get to the end. I was carrying something that weighed a ton, and I couldn't get rid of it − even though I didn't know what it was.

I suppose the dreams meant that I was scared stiff about the future. How would I manage? What would I do after I was sixteen and I wasn't at Tinley Road any more?

I almost gave up bothering about my clothes, and my hair, and my nails. What did it matter what I looked like? I was so ugly.

All lumpy, with huge tits that ached. I didn't bother with make-up any more. Who was going to fancy me the way I was?

I even missed my mum. At least if someone is ordering you around all the time you know that you're needed. And she always gave me enough money to buy clothes and make-up.

"I don't want the neighbours thinking I can't afford to keep you looking decent," she'd say.

When I showed her what I'd bought she'd always say something like, "I'd have thought green would be a better colour for you", or "I can't believe that a poorly-made top like that could cost such a lot", but at least she was there to say something.

Now nobody said anything to me – except when I was in school.

School was OK.

But it finished at three – and it was such a long time until nine the next morning.

Chapter 7
Hospital

I liked Tanya. I was sorry when she left Tinley Road, with Jade tucked under her arm like a parcel.

"Bye, Pinkie," she said as she left me and Tinley Road behind.

Tanya was a laugh. She and I used to creep out behind the back of the building to have a sneaky fag together. I think Liz and Sue – she was one of the other teachers – knew we did, but Tanya liked to make a big thing about it.

When Tanya went it seemed much quieter. I mostly chatted to Jackie – she was only fourteen, but she was OK. We talked about blokes mostly. I told her Phil had vanished into the great blue yonder as soon as I'd said the word "baby", just like Mum said he would. Jackie said her guy, Tom, was sticking by her. It was quite sweet – he was only fourteen too.

One day she asked April what had happened to her baby's dad. April went bright pink and said he'd gone away somewhere. Jackie said, "Typical bloke", and then went on telling me how she and Tom were going to get a flat together one day. I listened, but I didn't think it would happen. Tom's a bloke too.

We had all the ordinary sort of lessons, and then we had to learn all about babies. I didn't listen much. Zak was going to be the perfect baby.

Jackie and I larked about, and Cherry who always thought she was a laugh held the plastic baby under water until it filled up and sank. But April took it SO seriously.

We did cooking too, although when I took my macaroni cheese home Mum wouldn't let the little ones eat it. Nick said it smelt OK, but Mum said anything that came from a place full of slutty girls was bound to be full of germs. She threw it in the bin.

I didn't take anything home after that. I just left it in the kitchen at the Centre. The dishes were always washed up and neatly stacked away the next day, so someone must have dealt with it.

One day we had an argument about who made the best pastry. April suddenly said, "Pinkie made a lovely cheese flan last week. It was fantastic!"

We all stopped and looked at her, and she went pink.

"How do YOU know?" Jackie said. "You been licking up the crumbs?"

April hid her face with her hands, and she was so red she was glowing. Jackie was about to say something else, but Liz cut in. "Pinkie left it behind," she said, "so I had a piece. April was still here so she had one too. Didn't you, April? And she's right. It was delicious."

And April nodded, and nodded.

Jackie opened her mouth again, but I stopped her.

I didn't mean to.

It just happened.

I fainted.

****

April: It was scary when Pinkie fainted.

One minute she was sitting on the edge of the table talking to Jackie, and the next – CRASH! Pinkie was lying on the floor, and her face was a funny colour. Liz and Sue came rushing in. They took one look at her and called an ambulance.

Cherry tried to tell them that if someone faints then you should sit them up with their head between their legs, but Liz said no. This was different.

Pinkie went on lying there until the ambulance came, when she was carried off to hospital.

No-one rushed away after school. We were all hoping there'd be some news about Pinkie.

Jackie was sure that she'd be fine. Jem told us a story about an aunt of hers who fainted every week until her baby was born.

Hannah thought Pinkie had been looking ill all week. Cherry said no, she'd been looking fine.

But there was no news.

The others trailed off home, and Hannah and Jem went shopping.

I stayed to help clear up the cookery stuff. I quite often did that. It wasn't because I wanted to be Miss Helpful. It was because the hostel was so cold and lonely.

Sometimes Liz would make a cup of tea, and we'd sit and chat for a bit before we started sorting out the mess. She was OK. She didn't ask questions the way Sue did. "Where did you live? What happened with your Mum? Where's your boyfriend?"

I never told anyone about Marco. I never told them that he'd run away when I told him about the baby. Really, truly ran away! He stuffed everything into a backpack and ran off somewhere. I don't know where.

If anyone asked me who the baby's father was, I just shrugged. It didn't matter, anyway. Mum thought I'd been sleeping with so many boys that I didn't know who it was anyway, and she was never going to change her mind. She thought Marco had run away because he'd found out the kind of girl I was. I tried to say that he wasn't as nice as she thought and she slapped me. So that was that. If she didn't believe me, why would anyone else?

The day Pinkie fainted Liz and I made toast. That was a treat. We'd only done that a couple of times. And then the phone rang, and Liz answered it.

When she came back she was looking worried. "They're keeping Pinkie in hospital," she said. "They're going to operate on her. They're going to have to do an emergency Caesarean."

I didn't know what to say. In the end I just said, "Poor Pinkie. Poor baby."

Liz nodded. "Yes."

"She'll be OK, though," I said, and I sighed. "She's so strong. I wish I was like her."

Liz gave me an odd look, but all she said was, "Do you?"

And then she picked up a dustpan and brush and we had to get busy.

Chapter 8
Plastic Box

I don't remember fainting.

I don't remember much about waking up in hospital either. I remember what a shock it was when I found myself feeling all flat and empty, and how weird it was when a nurse came and told me that I had a little baby boy.

"That's Zak," I said, and she said it was a nice name. Then she said he wasn't very well, and that when I felt strong enough she'd take me to see him.

I stared at her. She thought I hadn't understood, so she said it again. "Pauline dear, your little boy's not very well. When you feel up to it we'll pop you in a wheelchair and take you down to see him."

I told her it was a mistake. My Zak was perfect. I knew he was perfect.

The nurse gave a little sigh, and then she helped me sit up in bed. My stomach was SO sore, but I didn't care. I just wanted to see Zak. They'd got him muddled up with another baby. They must have done. I wanted them to sort it out.

And I wanted to hold him and cuddle him, and watch his little face light up when he saw me. Me, his special friend.

But when I did see him I knew they were right. It was my baby ...

But it wasn't how I'd imagined Zak.

I knew it was mine because it looked like Phil. It was so weird, but he did – like a shrivelled and shrunken sort of Phil. He looked like a scrawny little, plucked chicken with Phil's face.

His eyes were screwed up, but his little chicken arms and legs were waving about as if he was trying to swim. And he was in this plastic box with tubes all over him, and there was a machine making him breathe.

All around him things were ticking, and little coloured lights were winking, and tubes were puffing and squishing. And it was so hot, but someone had put this stupid little hat on his head so he looked like a very, very old Phil.

I looked at him and I didn't feel anything.

No, that isn't true.

I looked at him and thought, he's horrible and ugly.

A doctor came to talk to me. I didn't understand what she said, except that Zak's heart had got something wrong with it. He'd have to be in the plastic box for a while. They'd try operating when he was bigger. She said he was being fed by a tube, but that he could have my milk if I wanted. I didn't know what she meant, and when she told me what I'd have to do, I said no. She said I could put my hand through a hole in the plastic box and touch him, but I didn't want to.

I couldn't believe that baby with all the tubes in him was anything to do with me. I sat in my wheelchair and stared and stared at him, but it didn't make sense. It was like watching an alien. Something from outer space.

And then he opened his eyes. Just for a second. He looked at me. And it was so *not* what I'd imagined that I had to turn the wheelchair round and move away.

A nurse came to wheel me back to my bed. While we were trundling down the corridor I found myself putting my hand on my stomach to feel Zak bouncing about inside me, and there was nothing there. There were metal clips, and soreness, but no Zak. He'd gone and I didn't know where. And I felt – nothing.

I stayed in hospital until I was ready to go home, and Mum and Nick came to collect me. Nick said something about Mum being the youngest grandma ever, and she nearly snapped his head off. She wouldn't speak to him all the way home. They didn't say much about Zak either. Maybe that was because I didn't want to talk about him. I don't know if they even went to look at him.

Someone from the hospital kept coming round to talk to me, but I said I didn't want to see them.

Then I went back to Tinley Road, and I made sure that I looked the best I'd ever looked.

I spent ages in the bathroom. It was weird, because Mum didn't bang on the door to shout at me like she usually did. She just left me to get on with it.

I dyed my hair the brightest pink you've ever seen. I threaded beads and spangles and sparkles on the long bits.

I looked great.

When I came downstairs Mum just shook her head, but she didn't say anything.

Nick said he'd take me to the Centre by car for the first few days. I said it was OK, I'd take the bus.

Chapter 9
In the Street

I don't think Liz and the school were expecting Pinkie back so soon. They looked so surprised when she burst in through the door it was funny.

Pinkie was smiling all over, and she asked everyone if they'd missed her. She even asked me, although she didn't wait for me to answer before she bounced across the classroom to talk to Jackie and Jem.

Liz asked Pinkie how Zak was, and she shrugged. She said – and she sounded so offhand – he'd be in hospital for ages yet. Then she began talking nineteen to the dozen, all about this boy she'd met in the hospital lift, and how he really fancied her and she liked him too. She said she was going to meet him after school, and she was going to do all her exercises so she'd be thin and gorgeous.

She was really chatty all day. And the next day. And the next. And she giggled in maths with Jackie, and dropped a bag of flour in cookery, and when she laughed it was SO

loud it began to hurt my head. She was mad.
Shouting jokes. Falling about. She couldn't
wait to get out of school at three o'clock.
If anyone got in her way she'd shove them
against the wall. Jackie said the boy she was
meeting must be really something.

****

On the Friday of that week I met her in
the street on the way to school. I didn't
mean to – I was usually early, but I was
feeling a bit odd that morning. Anyway, we
walked down the road together, and for once
Pinkie was quiet. We didn't talk at all.

I'd been thinking and thinking about her
and how she must feel about having an ill
baby, and as we got to the gate I made myself

say, "I'm sorry about Zak. I hope he's better soon – "

And she turned on me, and it was like the last time, only worse.

She said it wasn't any of my ****ing business, and I was to keep my nose out of her life and she couldn't wait to leave school because then she wouldn't have to see my ****ing face again.

It was so horrible that I couldn't help crying. And that made her start all over again, and she began ranting on about my trainers always being so white and my hair being so clean and shiny, and all the stuff she said before about me thinking I was better than her.

My breath stuck in my chest, and I thought she was going to hit me –

And she suddenly turned round and slammed off down the road.

Liz found me crying in the toilets. I didn't tell her what Pinkie had said, but Liz guessed it was something to do with her.

All she said was, "Maybe she needs a little time on her own."

And that afternoon my waters broke, and Julie drove me to the hospital.

And Lee was born.

I forgot about being scared and it hurting just as soon as they put him in my arms.

****

He was the most beautiful thing that had ever, ever happened to me. I wish I could say properly how beautiful he was, but I don't have the right kind of words. All I can say is that it was like I had every treasure in all the world for my very own, and the bottom of my stomach melted away because I loved him so much.

Chapter 10
Intensive Care

They said I could go home from the hospital the day after Lee was born, but when they heard about the hostel they said I had to stay longer. I didn't mind. Everyone was very nice to me, and Liz and Sue came in to see me.

Mum didn't come, but she did send a card.

I had times when Lee was asleep in his little cot so I wandered round the hospital a bit.

I found out where the Intensive Care ward was, and I wondered about going to see Zak. I was so full of loving for Lee that I felt a little bit the same for all the babies in the world. Especially the ill ones.

So I went to find Zak. It was late in the afternoon, but not quite visiting time, so I thought it would be quiet. I went up in the lift to the third floor, and then along the corridor. I found I was creeping along, as if I was doing something wrong. I couldn't help it.

The ward had a glass wall. I suppose it was so that you could look in without disturbing the babies. I crept up to it, and peered in.

There was a row of see-through plastic boxes, and each one had a baby inside. There were masses of machines round each one — it looked scary.

I was surprised to see mums and dads in there as well as the nurses. I suppose they

were there because their babies were so ill.
I thought they'd have to wait for visiting
times.

I was just thinking I'd have to ask which
baby was Zak when I saw something.

I saw someone.

I saw Pinkie.

She was at the end. She was sitting and
staring at a baby in a plastic box, and her face
was so strange. She didn't look happy.
She didn't look sad. She looked – I don't know
how to explain it. She looked as if there was
nothing inside her head. Her eyes were
working, but nothing else was. She was just
staring and staring.

And as I watched, she got up and walked
out, and it was like she was wound up by
clockwork. She didn't see me.

I don't think she saw anything.

And as she walked away down the corridor two women were coming the other way. I saw them look at Pinkie's hair, and her clothes, and one said, "Just look at the state of that!"

The other one screwed her mouth up, and nodded. Then she said, "She's up here every day. That's her kid, the one in the corner. Got no more than she deserves, by the look of things."

Then they smiled tight, pleased little smiles at each other and went into the lift.

And I hope they rot in hell for that.

Chapter 11
Tinley Road Again

If I'm truthful I felt really bad when April came back to Tinley Road. The last time I'd seen her I'd shouted at her, so when she came back I tried not to be near her.

It's so weird.

If it had been anyone else I'd have said something like, 'Sorry, I've been a real cow', and I'd have given them a hug to show them I really, truly was sorry. But I couldn't do that with April. I don't know why, specially as in a sort of way, she'd helped. The wild fit I'd had disappeared – but maybe that wasn't to do with April after all. Maybe it was because I was tired.

Why was I tired?

It doesn't really matter.

April didn't say anything much when she came back, but she was different.

I don't know how to explain it.

Before she'd been like a very shiny, see-through china cup, the very posh sort that shatters if you just knock it. Now she didn't feel like that any more. She wasn't so breakable, if you see what I mean.

I think Liz and Sue noticed too.

They must have done, because of what happened next.

We didn't have assemblies or anything like that at the Centre, but Liz and Sue always came in at breaktime and had a cup of tea with us. That was when they told us anything we needed to know.

Anyway, about two weeks after April returned, Liz came into break with a piece of paper in her hand. "I've had a bit of an odd request," she said. "Do any of you know St Helen's High School?"

Jackie made a face. "Yeah," she said, "the kids from my school used to beat them up."

Liz grinned. "Well, now may be your chance to make up for that, Jackie. They're asking if two of you would consider going to talk to the year sevens and eights about what it's like to be a mum before you're sixteen."

Jackie snorted loudly. "You mean they want to have a good sneer, Miss. They think they're SO smart at that place." She turned on April. "You went there, didn't you?"

April flicked her hair back with her hand, and nodded. "I didn't like it much," she said.

"I don't think we should go," Hannah said. "Why do they want to know about us anyway? They're just being dead nosy if you ask me."

Sue coughed. She always coughed before she said anything. "I think that some young people don't know what hard work it is looking after a baby. They think it's all cute little clothes and pretty toys – rather like having an especially lovely doll."

Hannah made a rude noise. "They should try having Dean for the night," she said. "He never stops yelling."

"Exactly," Sue said. "But they don't know that."

"What you mean is," Jackie said, "they want us to tell them how awful it is so as they don't go off shagging each other without condoms and stuff."

Sue and Liz both laughed. "That's about it, Jackie," Liz said.

"Well," Jackie said, and she folded her arms, "I'm not going. I'm not having that lot staring at me." She swung round in her chair and pointed at me. "Send Pinkie, Miss. She's good at talking!"

"Yes!" Hannah said, and Jem cheered, and Cherry clapped loudly.

Sue coughed again, and the noise died down. "Thank you," she said, "and I'm sure that Pinkie would be excellent – but aren't you forgetting something? Pinkie's baby isn't at all well."

There was a little silence.

I couldn't bear it.

"I'll go," I said, and I laughed. "I can tell them all about being pregnant. And fainting off the table!"

Liz smiled. Then she said, "We were wondering if you'd like to go too, April. Things haven't been easy for you, but you've done really well. And Lee's a star example of a well-kept baby!"

April went very pink, and we all waited for her to say she couldn't possibly go. Or for her to burst into tears. But she didn't. I was SO surprised.

She said, "I'll go. But will it be all right for Lee?"

"We'll make sure it is," Sue said. "We'll come with you."

Chapter 12
Back to the Beginning

So that's how I come to be here. About to walk onstage. The stage in the hall of St Helen's School ... and I'm about to tell a crowd of kids what it's like to be a teenage mother.

But something is happening to me. Something very strange ...

My heart is pounding and thundering and battering the walls of my chest. It's going to burst through my ribs any second. There'll be me, Pinkie, splattered all over the walls. Little sparkles and flashes burst inside my eyes, but there's blackness swirling round the outside of me. It's a huge blackness waiting to gulp me up …

And the sea of faces in front of me is growing and growing. Thousands and thousands of faces with gaping mouths and huge eyes – and the eyes are staring at me – and I'm frozen.

I can't move. I can't speak and the eyes are swaying … to and fro … to and …

What?

Something's happening.

April's there beside me. She's pushed me onto a chair at the edge of the stage, and dumped Lee in my arms. I nearly drop him –

it's my arms that clutch his little, warm, wriggly body, not me.

But it jolts me. I snatch a gasping breath. Lee wriggles again, and I hold him tightly. It's for my sake, not his.

Then I hear her. April. She's talking – and her voice isn't the way I've ever heard April sound. She sounds angry. And the dizziness clears away from my head and my eyes and I see her, and I see what she's doing.

She's standing in the middle of the platform, and she's talking to those eyes. All those blank faces. She looks so skinny and pathetic in her sparkly little top and her bare stomach showing like chicken flesh and her spotless jeans and her snow-white trainers and – yes, I knew it. She's shaking back her hair. But she's talking. And I begin to hear what she's saying.

"Look at us," April says. "Me and Pinkie. Look at Pinkie. She's the one on the chair, the one with the baby. It's not her baby, it's mine. Pinkie's baby's in hospital. He's really, really ill, and Pinkie's been slogging to and fro to see him, and he's not getting any better.

"She's worn out. That's why she's not talking to you. It's not because she's scared of you. Pinkie's the bravest person I've ever met, and she's not scared of anything.

"It's me who's the scared one. I was so scared of having a baby I didn't sleep for weeks and weeks. It was only when I found out Pinkie was having a baby too that I began to sleep again.

"Why? Because Pinkie wasn't scared. She stuck out her stomach like she was proud, and that made me feel different. She was like a queen who's got all her money and her jewels and the very best kingdom in all the world stuffed inside her, and she wanted us all to know just how good she felt. I never got to be proud, but I stopped being so scared."

******

I can't believe what I'm hearing.
I hang on to Lee as if he's the only thing in the whole world that can save me. I think about me, and I think about April, and it's like a whole heap of muddled-up jigsaw puzzle pieces are whirling round and round in my brain.

Was THAT why she followed me?

How could it be true?

How could it?

But I'm not the Pinkie she's talking about.

I can't be.

I'm bad.

I know that now. I've known it ever since Zak was born. I'm horrible Pauline. Dirty Pauline. Pauline who was born because her mother got pregnant when she was fifteen.

Pauline the punishment.

Oh, I tried to escape. I tried SO hard. I really believed I could change into someone else, someone quite different. I thought I could be Pinkie. Pinkie, who lived her own life her own way. And Pinkie would be different – SO different. And I nearly did it ... nearly ... but it still got me. The punishment. I couldn't escape.

I was still Pauline – horrible, dirty, bad Pauline ...

But now I'm hearing April again.

****

"Do you know something? Something terrible?" April's voice is wobbling. "They think that Pinkie deserved what she got. A little, ill baby with tubes stuck down his throat and a plastic fish tank all round him. Well, I think people who think like that are *evil*. *They're* much, MUCH worse than we are. We made a mistake, and everybody does that sometimes."

April takes a step towards the edge of the platform. "That's true, isn't it? *Isn't it*? Put your hand up if you've never made a mistake. Go on! Show me!"

No-one moves.

"And nobody EVER deserves to have an ill baby. ESPECIALLY not someone like Pinkie."

****

As I listen to April, the jigsaw pieces click, one by one by one, into place.

That's why April gets to me.

No ...

That's why she USED to get to me.

I always thought she was sneering at me. Sneering like everyone else. Like Mum.

I always thought she was this super-shiny, super-clean girl – the girl who thought she was better than me – but all the time it was me. It was ME who thought I was dirt, but I didn't see it. I thought it was her, but it was me all the time.

But now she's telling me something different. She's telling me that I'm – what did she say? A real person. Someone beautiful.

Someone special. Not a horrible, dirty girl that deserves her poor, sick baby – just a girl who made a mistake. And whose mother did too …

And the huge, hard lump in the middle of my chest that hurts and hurts and hurts all night and all day, bursts …

I bury my face in Lee's soft, warm tummy and the tears soak into his woolly bunny jumper until April very gently takes him away, and gives me another tiny, snow-white tissue.

I look at it and I cry even more, and I can't stop, and the world is whirling round me and all I want is Zak, I want Zak, I want to tell him that I love him. I really, really do and he won't ever need to look at me like that again – as if he was so sad … so sad … so sorry for me.

And April hugs me. And I let her. And she gives me another little tissue, and then she looks worried and she flicks back her hair and she says, "Oh, no! I haven't got any more!"

And I don't say anything because I can't speak for crying, but I want to say so many things – that I'm sorry, and thank you, and I'm so glad she isn't perfect – and then I wipe my nose on my black velvet sleeve and Lee gurgles and April smiles at me.

Barrington Stoke would like to thank all its readers for commenting on the manuscript before publication and in particular:

Hamit Akyol
Ian Anderson
Janet Andrews
Noah Ashford
Stacey Bain
Andrew Beamish
Gary Beer
Charlie Bremner
Susan Brown
David Cairns
Mel Campbell
Kevin Canaver
Colin Cook
Jimbo Cousins
Georgia Dickson
Greg Downie
Abbie Ferguson
Daniel Garson
K. Golding
Becky Gomm

Daniel Gough
Vicky Guy
Sean Henderson
Vicky Hill
Daniel Hodgson
Matthew Hodgson
Margaret Hubbard
Claire Hughes
Kim Hughes
Loyce Ihunzwa
Emma Irvine
Sharon Jamieson
Michele Lang
Jessica Lo
Dean Loughton
Alice Louth
Sean McVeigh
Nat Melia
Deirdre Michaelucci
Joshua Mills

David Morris
William Philps
Sharlene Sibley
Chris Smith
Amy Speed
Melis Stevens
Karl Stevenson
Stacey Troy
Barbara-Ann Truman
Kelly Tweedie
Leeann Watson
Sarah Watson-Saunders
James West
Robert Wiebkin
Alexander Williamson
Luke Wilson
Siobhan Wood
Chris Young

Become a Consultant!

Would you like to give us feedback on our titles before they are published? Contact us at the email address below – we'd love to hear from you!

Email: info@barringtonstoke.co.uk
Website: www.barringtonstoke.co.uk

If you loved this book why don't you read ...

Walking with Rainbows

by Isla Dewar

ISBN 1-842991-30-2

"Stepping out with Briggsy was like walking with rainbows."

When Briggsy turns up at Minnie's school on that first Monday in April, Minnie knows he's not like the other boys. Briggsy's family travels with the fairground and he has never stayed in one place for very long. He may have missed out on school but he has learnt what life's all about. He shares his passions with Minnie, and she knows that time spent with Briggsy is going to change her life for ever.

You can order **Walking with Rainbows** directly from our website at **www.barringtonstoke.co.uk**

If you loved this book why
don't you read ...

Text Game

by Kate Cann

ISBN 1-842991-48-5

Everything's going great in Mel's life.
And the best bit's Ben. He's gorgeous, he's
fun and great to be with – she can't believe
he's going out with her. Then she starts
getting nasty text messages. They say Ben's
playing with her. They say he's going to
dump her. They say he's seeing someone
else. Are they just from some jealous
nutcase, like her friend Lisa says? Or are
they telling the truth?

You can order *Text Game* directly from our website
at **www.barringtonstoke.co.uk**